To my niece and nephew,

Maya and Milan

Crazy Joaquim

瘋子喬昆

Christian Beamish 著

吳泳霈 譯

朱正明 繪

Paulo lived with his family in a small house by the sea. He was eight years old. Every day after school Paulo walked home, passed the fishermen's boats on the harbor beach, through the marketplace where the farmers sold their fruits and vegetables, across the field with a crumbling stone wall and finally, passed the lighthouse where an old man named Joaquim was the lighthouse keeper.

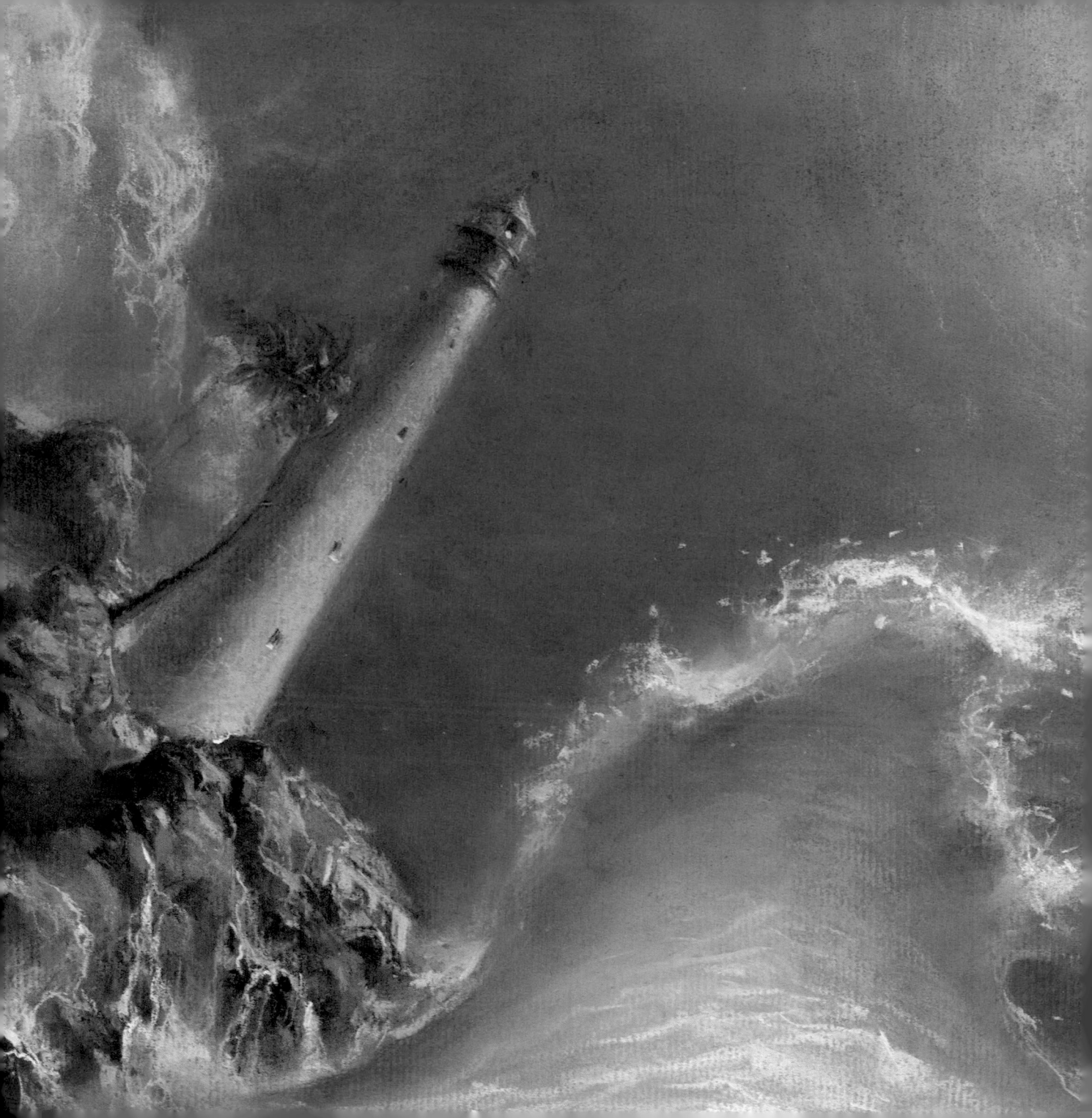

Paulo's brother, who was already old enough to go fishing with their father, said that the lighthouse keeper was crazy and that Paulo should stay away from him. The kids at school called the old man "Loco-Jo," by which they meant "Crazy Joaquim." Even Paulo's mother said that Joaquim was strange. "Why does he live out there all by himself? It isn't normal," she said.

Paulo was walking by the lighthouse one afternoon when he saw the old man working in the courtyard. The boy crept up to the rusted front gate of the lighthouse and crouched there, watching the old man. He looked fierce, Paulo thought. Gray stubble grew on the old man's chin and his silver hair stood wild and uncombed on his head. The old man was cutting a fishing net with a knife and he clenched his jaw tightly. The gate squeaked when Paulo leaned against it. The old man looked up and Paulo froze. The boy thought of running away, but he remained still.

"What are you doing?" the lighthouse keeper asked. His eyes were a very light blue, almost silver, and scary-looking.

"Nothing," Paulo answered from the other side of the rusted front gate.

The lighthouse keeper stood up from the table where he worked and walked toward Paulo. "What is your name?" the old man asked.

"Paulo," the boy replied.

"Well, Paulo, don't you know that it is rude to spy on people?"

"I did not mean to spy," Paulo said. "I was just watching you work."

The old man scratched his chin and put his hand on his hip. "I suppose that is different than spying," he said. The old man then asked Paulo, "Would you like to see the lighthouse?"

Paulo remembered what everyone had said, that the lighthouse keeper was crazy, that he was dangerous. The lighthouse keeper did look kind of scary with his silver eyes and gray whiskers and the wild hair standing on top of his head, but he was also very calm and polite. "Thank you," Paulo said, "I think I would like to see the lighthouse."

The boy and the old man climbed the thirteen turns of the creaking spiral staircase. At the top they stood on a black iron catwalk that circled the enormous glass lens of the light. Paulo saw the rocky shoreline far below and heard the surf crashing in. Joaquim pointed to dolphins swimming far out to sea. A school of tiny, silver fish darted through the water close to the rocks. Paulo saw the fishing boats on the harbor beach and his house in the distance and they looked very small, like toys.

"Let's go down to the cove beach and see what gifts the sea has brought us," the old lighthouse keeper said.

"Gifts the sea has brought?" Paulo asked.

"Why of course!" the old man exclaimed with his arms stretched out and his eyebrows raised.

Paulo wondered if the kids at school weren't right about the lighthouse keeper, if perhaps he wasn't really crazy after all.

"The sea brings something every day," Joaquim said, stooping down with his hands on his knees to look at Paulo. "Gifts, my friend," the old man said, "gifts." His bright eyes gleamed in the sun and the old man laughed. He then walked back down the spiral staircase and across the courtyard, and climbed down a thick wooden ladder to the cove below. "Come on!" he called.

Paulo followed.

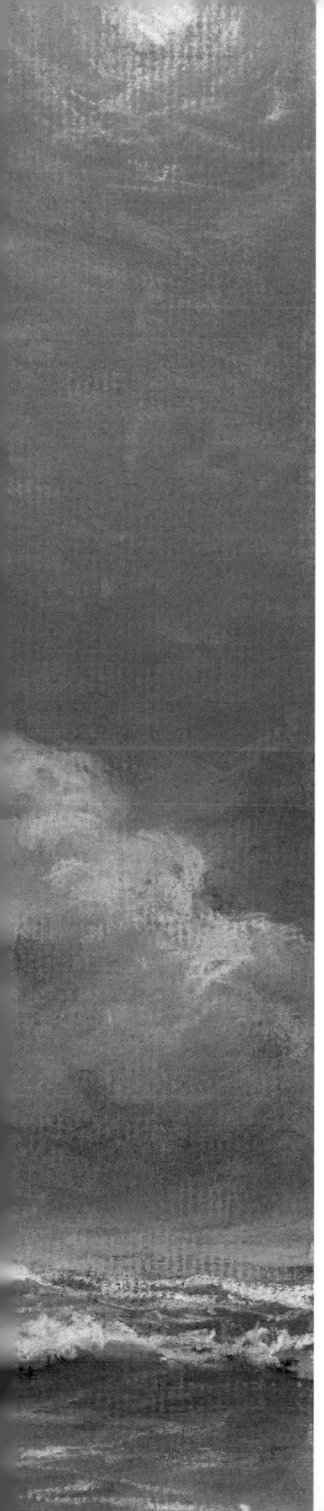

The old lighthouse keeper stepped quickly across the rocks. Paulo followed but he couldn't go as fast as the old man.

"What about the gifts from the sea?" Paulo asked, shielding his eyes from the sun. A small wave crashed on the rocks at Paulo's feet, then drained back into the sea.

"The gift is sunshine and blue sky!" the lighthouse keeper said, laughing.

"That's not much of a gift," Paulo said, sticking his hands in the pockets of his trousers as the sea rushed in again.

"We might find something yet," Joaquim said, smiling his fierce but friendly smile, and searching the cobblestones.

After a while, the lighthouse keeper and Paulo walked back across the cove.

When the boy climbed back up the ladder to the courtyard, he said, "Maybe you will have better luck finding gifts tomorrow."

"What do you mean, my friend?" the old man asked. "I found a gift today." The old man held out his hand and showed Paulo a round piece of smooth, blue sea glass. "It is for you, young man."

Paulo took the piece of sea glass and ran his thumb over the round edge, then held it up to his eye like a lens and looked at the lighthouse and saw it turn blue. Paulo smiled.

"You can come back tomorrow," the lighthouse keeper said, "and we'll drill a hole and run a string through so you can keep the glass around your neck."

"I would like that," Paulo said. He held the glass up to his eye once more and looked at the old man in blue light.

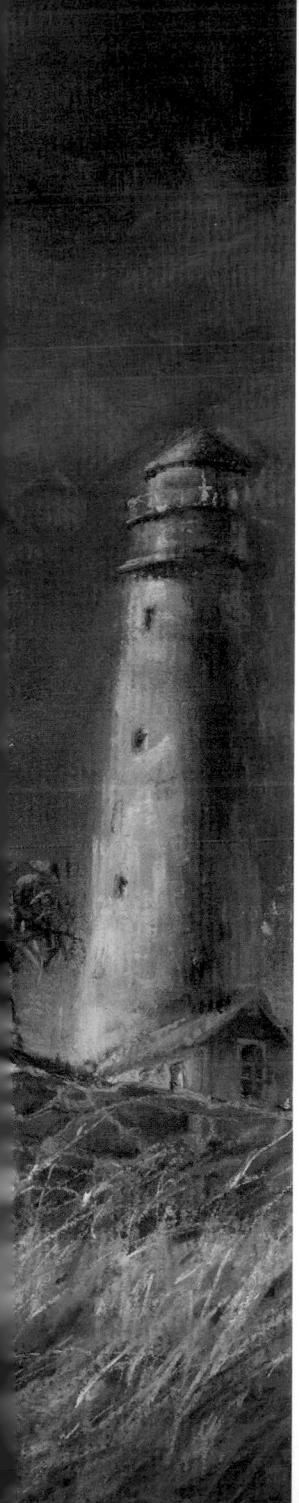

They walked across the courtyard and shook hands. Paulo walked through the rusted front gate and started down the path to his house. He stopped and turned around to look at the lighthouse and wave to the lighthouse keeper. "Thanks for the glass, see you tomorrow!" Paulo yelled.

The old man waved and said, "O.K., see you tomorrow!"

As Paulo walked a little further, he wondered what he would say to his family and to the kids at school about meeting the old lighthouse keeper that they called, "Crazy Joaquim."

Vocabulary

p.10

whisker [`hwɪskɚ] n. （常用複數）鬢鬚

p.13

trellis [`trɛlɪs] n. 棚架式涼亭

canopy [`kænəpɪ] n. 遮篷

bleach [blitʃ] v. 漂白，使……變白

arc [ɑrk] v. 形成弧形

saber [`sebɚ] n. 軍刀

olive [`ɑlɪv] n. 橄欖

rail [rel] n. 橫桿

ashore [ə`ʃor] adv. 在岸上

cove [kov] v. 小海灣

p.14

creak [krik] v. 嘎吱作響

spiral [`spaɪrəl] adj. 螺旋形的

staircase [`stɛr,kes] n. 樓梯

catwalk [`kæt,wɔk] n. 狹窄小道

dart [dɑrt] v. 突進，猛衝

p.21

stoop [stup] v. 俯身，彎腰

gleam [glim] v. 閃爍

p.23

shield [ʃild] v. 遮蔽

cobblestone [`kɑbl̩,ston] n. 鵝卵石

p.24

sea glass　海玻璃

故事中譯

P.2

　　八歲的保羅和他的家人住在一間靠海的小房子裡。保羅每天放學走路回家的途中，會經過停靠漁船的港口、穿越農夫們販賣蔬菜水果的市集和一片有面碎石牆的野地，最後則會經過一座燈塔。這座燈塔的看守員是一位名叫喬昆的老人。

P.5

　　保羅有個已經大得可以和父親一起出海捕魚的哥哥，他說那個燈塔看守人是個瘋子，叫保羅要離他遠一點。學校裡的小朋友也都叫這個老人「瘋老喬」，意思是「發瘋的喬昆」。就連保羅的母親也覺得喬昆很奇怪。她說：「為什麼他要獨自一個人住在燈塔裡？真是不正常。」

P.6

　　有一天下午保羅經過燈塔時，看到老人正在燈塔前的庭院裡工作，於是他便悄悄走到燈塔生鏽的前門那兒，蹲著觀察老人。保羅心想：「這個老人看起來好兇狠喔。」他的下巴長滿了灰色的短鬚，一頭銀色白髮凌亂而未梳理。他緊咬著牙根，正在用小刀割斷一張漁網。當保羅倚靠在柵門上時，門突然嘎嘎作響。老人抬頭看他，保羅嚇得全身僵硬。他想要逃跑，但卻一動也不能動。

P.8

　　燈塔看守人問保羅：「你在做什麼？」他那雙淡到接近銀色的淺藍色眼睛看起來有點嚇人。

保羅從生鏽的前門另一邊回答：「沒有。」

燈塔看守人從他工作的桌子旁站起來走向保羅，問他：「你叫什麼名字？」

男孩回答：「保羅。」

「保羅，你不知道偷看別人是不禮貌的行為嗎？」

保羅回答：「我不是有意要偷看，我只是在觀察你工作而已。」

p.10

老人搔了搔下巴思考著，然後將手放在腰下，說：「我想那和偷看是不一樣的。」接著他問：「你想參觀燈塔嗎？」

保羅回想起大家說過的話——燈塔看守人是個瘋子，他很危險——這個燈塔看守人那對銀色的眼睛、滿臉的灰色鬍鬚及一頭凌亂豎起的頭髮，看起來的確有點嚇人；不過，他卻非常沉著有禮。保羅回答：「謝謝你，我很樂意參觀燈塔！」

p.13

老人為男孩打開前門，他們穿過燈塔庭院裡的石板路。庭院裡有一個老人自己搭建的竹棚，上面覆蓋著紅色及黃色的帆船布來遮陽。兩根在日曬之下變得又乾又白的鯨魚肋骨，像兩把交叉著的軍刀，成弧形立在燈塔的門上。燈塔看守人在老舊的橄欖油罐子裡種了一些紅花和藍花；他還利用漁船殘骸的船圍做了一個長椅放在庭院裡。

喬昆伸手一揮，說：「這些被海浪沖上岸的東西，全都是我在燈塔下方的海灣岸邊發現的。來！我帶你參觀燈塔。」

P.14

男孩和老人沿著咯吱作響的螺旋梯攀爬了十三圈。到達塔頂後，他們站在鐵鑄的黑色狹窄通道上；這通道環繞著塔頂大燈外圍的巨大玻璃透鏡。保羅看著下方遙遠的岩岸，並聽著海浪撞擊岸邊的聲音。喬昆指著遠方正游向大海的海豚；一群銀白色的小魚突然急速游竄至岩岸邊的水域裡。保羅還看到遠處停靠在港口的漁船和他的家，它們看起來非常小，就像玩具一樣。

P.18

年老的燈塔看守人說：「讓我們到下面的海灣岸邊，看看大海為我們帶來了什麼禮物吧！」

保羅問：「大海會帶來禮物？」

老人伸開雙臂，揚起眉毛大聲說：「當然了！」

保羅開始懷疑，學校裡的小朋友是不是誤會了這個燈塔看守人？也許他根本就不是個瘋子。

P.21

喬昆說：「大海每天都會帶來一些東西。」他彎下身子，用手撐著膝蓋，看著保羅。老人說：「禮物，我的朋友。禮物。」他笑了，明亮的眼睛在陽光下閃爍著。然後他回頭走下螺旋梯，穿過庭院，爬下粗厚的木梯，到達下面的海灣。他對著保羅大喊：「來吧！」

保羅跟了上去。

P.23

年老的燈塔看守人快步穿越過岩石。保羅跟在後面，但卻無法走得跟老人一樣快。

保羅用手遮蔽刺眼的陽光，問：「從大海來的禮物呢？」一陣小小的波浪沖上他腳邊的岩石，然後再退回海裡。

燈塔看守人笑著說：「陽光和藍天就是禮物啊！」

保羅將手插進褲子的口袋裡說：「那不能算是禮物吧？」此時海浪又再次沖打進來。

喬昆說：「我們也許會發現其他東西！」他露出威嚴卻和善的笑容，並在鵝卵石之間尋找著。

P.24

過了一會兒，燈塔看守人和保羅往回走，穿越過這個小海灣。

當男孩爬上梯子、回到庭院時，他對老人說：「也許明天你的運氣會比較好，能發現禮物。」

老人問：「我的朋友，你的意思是什麼呢？我今天就發現一個禮物了！」老人伸出他的手，給保羅看一塊圓滑的藍色海玻璃。「年輕人，這是給你的！」

p.26

保羅拿著這塊海玻璃，用大拇指輕輕滑過圓滑的玻璃邊緣，然後將它舉到眼前，當作透鏡一樣欣賞著；透過海玻璃，他看到燈塔變成了藍色。保羅微微一笑。

燈塔看守人說：「你明天可以再來。我們在海玻璃上鑽一個小洞，然後穿上一條線，這樣你就可以把它掛在脖子上。」

保羅說：「好啊！」他再次將玻璃湊到眼前，看著老人籠罩在藍光中。

p.29

他們走過庭院，握手道別。保羅穿過生鏽的前門，邁向通往他家的小徑。他停下腳步，轉身看著燈塔並向燈塔看守人揮手，叫著：「謝謝你的海玻璃！明天見！」

老人揮手回答：「好，明天見！」

p.30

保羅走了一小段路後，心裡想著要怎麼告訴家人及學校裡的小朋友，自己和年老的燈塔看守人——就是大家所稱的「瘋老喬」——的相遇。

Exercises

Part One. Reading Comprehension

Answer the following questions about the story in short sentences.

1. What did the kids at Paulo's school call Joaquim? What did they mean by that?

2. What was Joaquim's occupation?

3. What did Joaquim think Paulo was doing when he first saw Paulo?

4. Where did the things in the lighthouse courtyard come from?

5. What was "the gift the sea has brought" that day?

Part Two. Topics for Discussion

Answer the following questions in your own words and try to support your answers with details in the story. There are no correct answers to the questions in this section.

1. There's an old saying that goes, "Don't judge a book by its cover." What does it mean? Can you relate the saying to the story?

2. Joaquim said in the story, "*Let's go down to the cove beach and see what gifts the sea has brought us.*" In your opinion, what are the gifts the sea has brought us in our lives?

Answers

Part One. Reading Comprehension

1. They called him "Loco-jo," by which they meant "Crazy Joaquim."
2. He was the lighthouse keeper.
3. He thought Paulo was spying on him.
4. They all came from the sea. Joaquim found them washed ashore in the cove below the lighthouse.
5. The gift was a piece of sea glass.

旅遊導覽

海上的巨人－燈塔

●燈塔的功用與變革

　　自古以來，燈塔一直肩負著在暗夜星沉，霧鎖洋面的天候裡，為迷途的船隻指引方向的任務。燈器與塔身為構成燈塔的兩大要件。因為燈塔的功能是指引海上船隻，所以多建造於鄰近海岸、視野遼闊之地，燈器要求光力強大，而塔身要求巨大堅固。隨著歲月的變遷，塔身經歷過木造、石造、磚造、鐵造，一直到今天用鋼筋混凝土的變革；而燈器也由最早的燃燒木材作為發光源，到蠟燭、油燈、煤氣燈，然後發展成現在的電燈。

●燈塔管理員

　　燈塔管理員是一項專業的技術性工作，他們必須對各種助航設備有深入的了解，並負責保養修繕燈器，以確保燈器在海上照明的功能。而燈塔多半地處偏遠，除了偶爾路過的船隻外，根本不見人影，因此除了看守燈塔的工作外，他們得學會自己打發時間，來度過日夜僅有燈塔為伴的日子。對於這些將生命與歲月奉獻給海洋與船隻的燈塔管理員，我們該給予他們多幾分敬意才是。

> 某些燈塔的位置過於偏僻，若遇上持續多天暴風雨，燈塔管理員可能會面臨食物短缺的問題。曾有過燈塔管理員以吃蠟燭捱過困境的例子出現，不過當時的蠟燭是由食用油做成。

●燈塔之最

1. 最早的燈塔——「法魯司島燈塔」(The Pharos of Alexandria) 是文獻上有記載最早的燈塔，建於西元前 305 年埃及西北部亞歷山卓港附近，規模壯觀，曾被譽為「世界七大奇蹟」之一，但卻毀於西元 1326 年的一場大地震。

2. 現存最古老的燈塔——「海克力斯燈塔」(The Tower of Hercules)，位於西班牙西北柯魯納海岸，約於西元前 20 年建造，至今仍可使用。

3. 最高的燈塔——「橫濱塔」(Yokohama Marine Tower)，位於日本橫濱山下公園附近，高 106 公尺。

4. 最美麗的燈塔——「費司南特燈塔」(Fastnet Lighthouse)，位於愛爾蘭西南方孤島上，有「愛爾蘭的眼淚」(The Teardrop of Ireland) 之稱。

5. 台灣最東邊的燈塔——台東蘭嶼燈塔
　　最西邊的燈塔——金門東椗島燈塔 (台灣區最西為澎湖花嶼燈塔)
　　最北邊的燈塔——連江東引島燈塔 (台灣區最北為基隆彭佳嶼燈塔)
　　最南邊的燈塔——屏東恆春鵝鑾鼻燈塔

●台灣燈塔——鵝鑾鼻燈塔

　　全台灣的燈塔共有 35 座，其中以墾丁的鵝鑾鼻燈塔最為大家所知。鵝鑾鼻燈塔建於清光緒七年，因為原住民不斷滋擾，清廷還派遣官兵守衛，讓這座燈塔成為全世界獨一無二的「武裝燈塔」。同時，它所發出的光力高達一百八十萬隻燭光，為亞洲之冠，有「東亞之光」的美譽。燈塔目前有人看守，並開放民眾參觀。

●結語

　　由於科技發達，精密的電子儀器以及衛星導航系統，已經取代了燈塔的地位，幫助船隻更為準確的指引方向。雖說燈塔的地位已經不如過去，但無可否認的，它在人類的航海史上，仍開啟了重要的新頁。

About the Author

Born March 15th, 1969 in Laguna Beach, Christian Beamish has always been attracted to the water. His father introduced him to the ocean at a very young age and he has been surfing for more than 25 years. In 1987, after graduating high school, Christian joined the U.S. Navy and worked in a construction battalion on many overseas projects. His Navy travels have been a very important part of his development as a writer since he was exposed to many interesting places and people. The time he spent in Cape Verde with the Navy was the basis for the Paulo and Joaquim stories: the unique culture of the islands and the way the people there are so closely connected to the sea. Christian currently lives in San Clemente, California and has plans to build an 18-foot sailboat for the next stage of his ocean development.

Author's Note: About *Crazy Joaquim*

I visited Cape Verde in 1991 as a construction worker with the U.S. Navy. We built a school in the capital city of Praia on the island of Santiago. Almost every evening after work I walked out to swim off the point where a beautiful lighthouse stood. Eventually, I met the lighthouse keeper and he showed me the tower. Although that man was not exactly like the character Joaquim in the story, he was very kind and lived alone. I imagined a young boy discovering the importance of judging people for himself, based on his own experiences despite what other people say. After writing this story I had an opportunity to live and work at Pigeon Point Lighthouse in Pescadero, California—it's a beautiful place and I think Paulo and Joaquim would think so too!

關於繪者

朱正明

1959 年次，現居台北市。

年幼好塗鴉；自高中時期即選讀美工科，業畢次年 (1979) 考取國立藝術專科學校美術科西畫組，1982 年以西畫水彩類第一名畢業。

求學時期除水彩、素描技法之外，並對漫畫、卡通之藝術表現形式頗有興趣，役畢後工作項度側重於卡通、漫畫、插畫。

1999 年驟生再學之念，並於次年考取國立師範大學美術研究所西畫創作組；2003 年取得美術碩士學位，該年申請入師大附中實習教師獲准，次年 2004 年取得教育部頒發之美術科正式教師資格證書，目前仍為自由工作者身分。

愛閱雙語叢書

(具國中以上英文閱讀能力者適讀)

祕密基地系列

Paulo, Joaquim and the Lighthouse Series

Christian Beamish　著

吳泳霈　譯

朱正明　繪

中英雙語，全套五本，附英文朗讀CD

① Crazy Joaquim　瘋子喬昆
② Paulo Joins the Fleet　第一次捕魚
③ The Apology　保羅的道歉
④ Homecoming　歸來
⑤ The Blue Marlin Festival　藍馬林魚節

一段發生在西非的島嶼上，關於友誼與成長的故事。

在西非外海小島上的海邊漁村，矗立著一座
燈塔。燈塔管理員是一個叫喬昆的獨居老
人，村民們都誤以為他是個瘋子，但八歲
的小男孩保羅卻和他成為忘年之交，並學
到許多人生哲理。本系列五個溫馨且具
啟發性的生活事件，紀錄喬昆和保羅的
友誼。清新雋永的文字，配上細緻優
美的插畫，值得您細細品味。

愛閱雙語叢書

世界故事集系列

你想知道，
如何用簡單的英文，
說出一個個耳熟能詳的故事嗎？
本系列改編自世界各國民間故事，
讓你體驗以另一種語言呈現
你所熟知的故事。

Jonathan Augustine 著

Machi Takagi 繪

Bedtime Wishes
睡前願望

The Land of the
Immortals
仙人之谷

國家圖書館出版品預行編目資料

Crazy Joaquim:瘋子喬昆 / Christian Beamish著;朱正明繪;吳泳霈譯.－－初版一刷.－－臺北市: 三民, 2005
面; 公分.－－(愛閱雙語叢書.祕密基地系列①)
ISBN 957–14–4332–8　（精裝）

1.英國語言－讀本

524.38　　　　　　　　　　　　　94012752

網路書店位址　http://www.sanmin.com.tw

© Crazy Joaquim
——瘋子喬昆

著作人	Christian Beamish
繪　者	朱正明
譯　者	吳泳霈
發行人	劉振強
著作財產權人	三民書局股份有限公司 臺北市復興北路386號
發行所	三民書局股份有限公司 地址／臺北市復興北路386號 電話／(02)25006600 郵撥／0009998–5
印刷所	三民書局股份有限公司
門市部	復北店／臺北市復興北路386號 重南店／臺北市重慶南路一段61號

初版一刷　2005年8月
編　號　S 805661
定　價　新臺幣貳佰元整
行政院新聞局登記證局版臺業字第○二○○號

有著作權，不准侵害

ISBN　957–14–4332–8　（精裝）